Dexter the Dog an

Dexter Makes New Friends

by Tonya Wilhelm

illustrated by Yadrikhinskaya Elsa

DEXTER THE DOG AND FRIENDS

Dexter Makes New Friends

Copyright © 2022 Tonya Wilhelm

Illustrator Yadrikhinskaya Elsa

Editor Kate Richards

ISBN: 9781082086335

Printed in the United States of America

Dedicated to Dexter.

"Dexter, today is going to be an extraordinary day.
I know moving to a new home can be scary.
I will always be by your side," stated Dexter's mom.

"Today, we are going to go to the park and make new friends," said Dexter's mom.

"Hi, my name is Levi. What's your name," asked Levi.

"My name is Dexter. My mom and I just moved here from Michigan," answered Dexter.

"It's nice to meet you, Dexter. Why did your mom bring a stroller to the dog park?" asked Levi.

"When I was born, my brain didn't grow right. I have a disease called Chiari Malformation.
Pronounced Kee-ah-ree," explained Dexter.

"Because of my unique brain, I get tired a lot and can't always walk right.

When my body is tired, my mom will put me in my stroller so I can rest."

"Even though I have days where I don't feel well,
I can still do many fun things," Dexter said.

"This is Maddie," Levi announced.

"Hi, Dexter. Did you know Michigan has over 10,000 lakes and has the longest freshwater shoreline in the world?" inquired Maddie.

"No. I did not know that. Thank you for sharing that fun fact," Dexter laughed.

Levi yelled, "PENNY! SLOW DOWN!"

"This is Penny Dane," Levi woofed.

"Hello. I'm Penny, otherwise known as Slow Down Penny," Penny barked.

"Hi, Penny," Dexter giggled.

"It really is nice of you to introduce me to your friends," said Dexter.

"That's what friends are for," explained Levi.

"Dexter, this is Trixie and her little brother Haru," woofed Levi.

"Hi, Dexter. Welcome to the neighborhood," barked Trixie.

"Hi, Dex," woofed Haru.

"Hi, Trixie and Haru. It's nice to meet you," Dexter said.

"I'm lucky to have you as my new friend," barked Dexter.

"I think we are going to be best friends forever," Levi said.

"You had a big day today. You look tired.
It's time to give your body a rest," said Dexter's mom.

"Goodbye, Levi."

"Bye, Dexter."

"I am glad you made such nice friends at the park. Tomorrow, we will go back to play with your new friends.

Good night, Dexter.

Always remember, I love you to the moon and back,"
said Dexter's mom.

Tonya and Dexter's Purpose

Tonya Wilhelm, a professional dog trainer based in Ohio, has always had a love for children. Tonya and her dog, Dexter, have visited numerous schools teaching children how to interact with dogs. Together, they don't just teach children how to properly greet dogs, but how to have fun with them, too!

Dexter is quite the trickster. He loves performing dog tricks with the children. Kids laugh and giggle as Dexter races around from one kid to another doing his tricks. Dexter loves to spin, roll over, and jump through hoops, but mostly eating treats.

Dexter, is a fun-loving Cavalier King Charles Spaniel that also has a neurological and mobility disability called Chiari malformation and syringomyelia. Chiari malformation is a condition in which the lower part of the brain extends into the spinal canal. This blocks the normal flow of the cerebrospinal fluid. The blockage then can cause fluid-filled pockets throughout the spinal cord, called syringomyelia. This disease is very common in the Cavalier King Charles Spaniel breed. With proper medications and physical therapy, Dexter lives a very happy life.

Dexter The Dog and Friends series follows Dexter through various stories and travels focusing on difficult topics such as disabilities, adoption, bullies, and death in an uplifting and inspiring manner. The books are about promoting acceptance, friendship, and living life to the fullest.

Doggone Fun

- You can stay up to date with Dexter's real life adventures and merchandise by visiting: www.Dexterthedogandfriends.com
- Raising Your Pets Naturally: Dog behavior, training, cat behavior, pet nutrition, pet care, pet product reviews and traveling with dogs. www.Raisingyourpetsnaturally.com
- Cavalier Gifts: Cavalier King Charles Spaniel gifts and merchandise. www.Cavaliergifts.com
- Dog Obsessed Shop: All breeds, all the time. www.Dogobsessedshop.com
- One more for good measure: www.Lifewithtonya.com

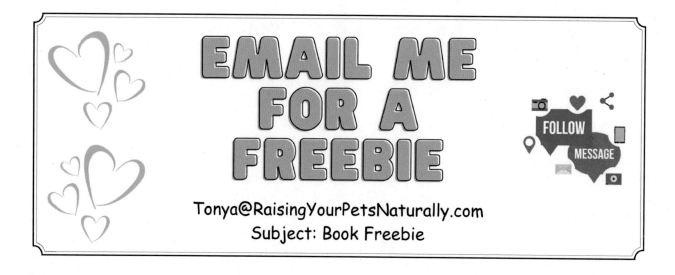

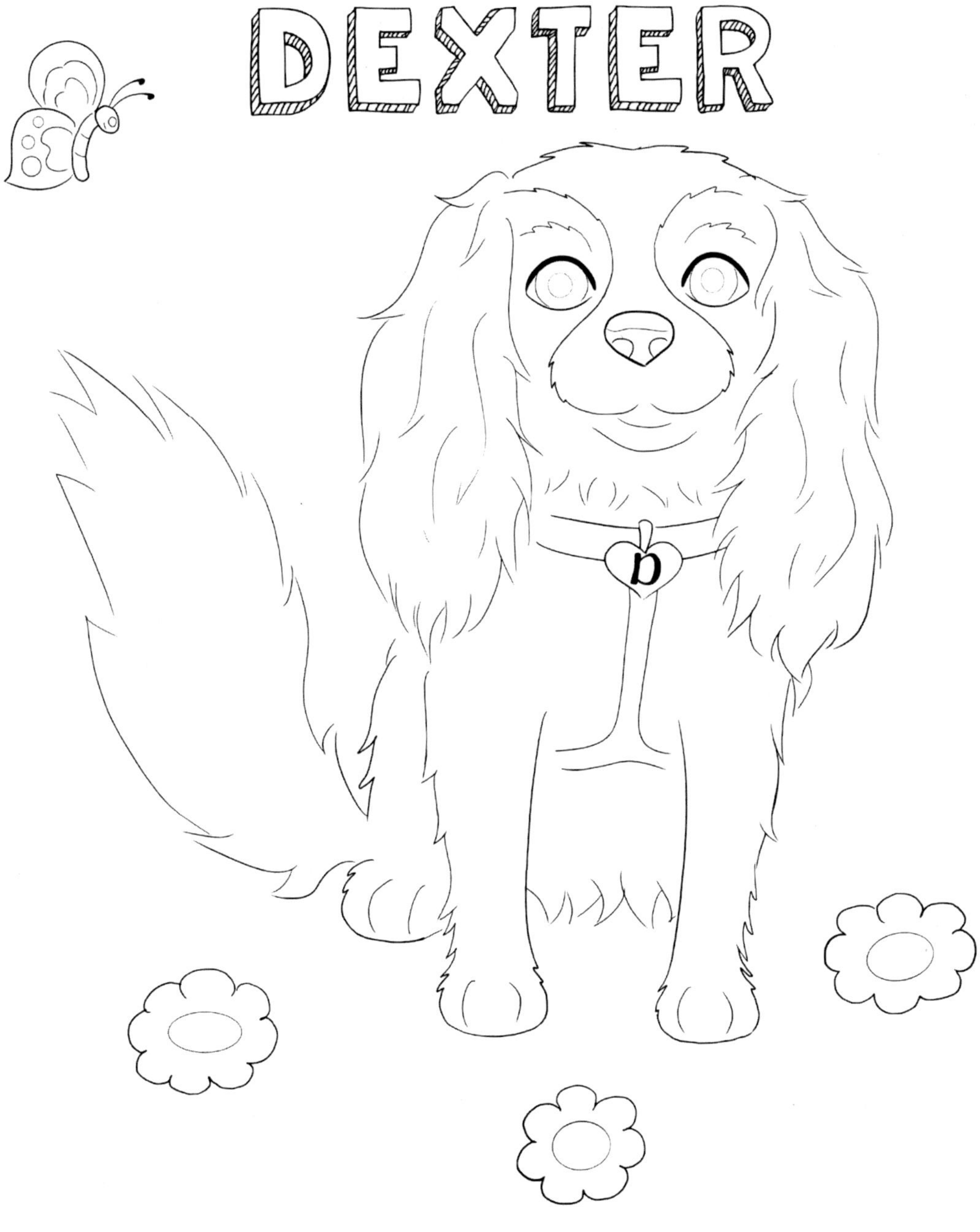
DEXTER
D

LEVI

PENNY

HARU

Made in the USA
Middletown, DE
25 July 2022